Bunny's Book Club

AUTHOR	Silvestro, Annie
ILLUSTRATOR	Mai-Wyss, Tatjana
TITLE	BUNNY'S BOOK CLUB

DATE DUE	BORROWER'S NAME
OCT 12	Bunny
NOV 09	BEAR
DEC 10	porcupine
JAN 02	raccoon

Silvestro, Annie

Mai-Wyss, Tatjana

Bunny's Book Club

For Joe, Sam, and Charlie,
my three favorite bookworms
–A.S.

To my family of book lovers
–T.M-W.

Text copyright © 2017 by Annie Silvestro
Cover art and interior illustrations copyright © 2017 by Tatjana Mai-Wyss
All rights reserved. Published in the United States by Doubleday,
an imprint of Random House Children's Books,
a division of Penguin Random House LLC, New York.

Doubleday and the colophon are registered trademarks
of Penguin Random House LLC.

Visit us on the Web! rhcbooks.com
Educators and librarians, for a variety of teaching tools,
visit us at RHTeachersLibrarians.com

Library of Congress Cataloging-in-Publication Data is available upon request.

ISBN 978-0-553-53758-1 (trade) — ISBN 978-0-553-53759-8 (lib. bdg.)
ISBN 978-0-553-53760-4 (ebook) — ISBN 978-0-375-97746-6 (premium)

Book design by Martha Rago
MANUFACTURED IN CHINA
10 9 8 7 6 5 4 3

Random House Children's Books supports the First Amendment
and celebrates the right to read.

This Imagination Library edition is published by Doubleday, an imprint of Random House Children's Books,
a division of Penguin Random House LLC, exclusively for Dolly Parton's Imagination Library, a not-for-profit
program designed to inspire a love of reading and learning, sponsored in part by The Dollywood Foundation.
Penguin Random House's trade editions of this work are available wherever books are sold.

Annie Silvestro

Bunny's Book Club

Illustrated by Tatjana Mai-Wyss

Doubleday Books for Young Readers

$\mathcal{B}$unny loved books.

He'd loved them ever since he first heard the lady with the red glasses reading aloud outside the library.

As he listened, Bunny
imagined himself climbing
mountains . . .

captaining a ship . . .

ruling a
kingdom. . . .

But when summer ended, story time moved back inside.
Bunny wasn't sure if animals were allowed in the library.
But Bunny *was* sure he couldn't live without books.

Night after night, he could hardly sleep for wishing.

He had to do something.

So, with a flashlight in his paws and hope in his heart,
Bunny jumped out of bed and tiptoed through the dark.

But when he reached the library door, it was locked. So were the windows.

Bunny tried digging, climbing, and yanking. Nothing worked.

Until finally he noticed . . .

. . . the book return!

The shiny handle was far above his head. But it was no
match for a high-hopping Bunny hungry for books.

Bunny leapt.

He clung to the bar, flung himself over, and wriggled his cottontail through the slot.

He landed inside with a **THUD**.

Bunny's eyes sparkled
at the sight of the shelves
bursting with books.

It was better than a field
full of fresh, crunchy carrots!

Bunny didn't know where to start.

He took a deep breath. It smelled as if he were wrapped inside the pages of his favorite book.

He followed his nose to the adventure section.

There he found stories about

swashbucklers,

sharks, and superheroes!

Bunny greedily grabbed them all.

His whiskers twitching with excitement, he slipped
his treasures through the book slot, one by one.

Then, performing his best balancing act, Bunny wobbled home. He couldn't wait to dig in.

And so Bunny returned to the library each night.
He searched and sneaked, then scurried back to read.

Soon, his home was more books than burrow!

Then one evening, a loud knock startled Bunny. He closed his book and opened the door.

"Where have you been?" asked Porcupine.

"Reading," said Bunny.

"Why?" said Porcupine.

Bunny's eyes popped wide open.

"Why?" he sputtered. "Have you ever been to the library?"

It was time for Bunny to let Porcupine in on his secret.

"Are you sure this is a good idea?" said Porcupine.
"Calm your quills," said Bunny.
"I'm too prickly—I'll never fit!"

Bunny pushed and shoved until . . .
POP went Porcupine.
Bunny slipped in and flipped on his flashlight.

"Whoa," said Porcupine.

"I know," said Bunny.

"Do you think there's a story about balloons?
I've always wondered about balloons."

"Most definitely," said Bunny.

Sure enough, Porcupine
found books on balloons.

And on deserts and dunes,
on caterpillars and cocoons.

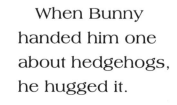

When Bunny
handed him one
about hedgehogs,
he hugged it.

The two friends took turns cramming books out the slot.
Their towers teetered so high, they could barely carry them.

Back at Bunny's, they cozied up with cups of tea and carrot muffins.

Together, they read until sunrise.

One night, Bear noticed the light on at Bunny's. He opened the door and tripped over a stack of books.

"What's going on?" said Bear.
"Here," said Bunny, handing him a book.

Bear made room and settled in to read.

Soon, more curious animals began visiting.

"Do you have any books about outer space?" said Bird.

Burrow sweet Burrow

"Or about volcanoes?" asked Mole.

"I'd like a ghost story," said Mouse.

"I think it's time for a field trip," said Bunny.

One by one, the animals stuffed themselves inside the library. (Bear caused a bit of a delay.)

They scattered about, sniffing the stacks, pawing over pages.

Squirrel gathered stories about the circus.

Raccoon nabbed one about outlaws and bandits.

Frog found a fairy tale.

No one heard the key in the front door.
No one heard the clack, clack, clacking of footsteps.
No one heard the light flick on.

"What do we have here?" said the librarian.
The animals looked up in shock.
Bunny gasped.
Porcupine gaped.
Bear groaned.

"Follow me," she said.
The animals marched slowly behind her.
"We're done for," whispered Porcupine.

"All libraries have rules," said the librarian sternly.
  Bunny's whiskers trembled.
    Porcupine's back bristled.
      Bear eyed the door.
        Bunny stepped forward to take the blame.

The librarian leaned down. . . .

"The first rule is: Every book lover must have one of these," she said.

She handed Bunny and his friends shiny new library cards.

"Now you may borrow books," she said, smiling. "As long as you return them, of course!"

Bunny couldn't believe his ears. They could keep coming to the library!

He beamed at his fellow readers,
then bounced to the shelves.
   He picked the perfect book.
   And he proudly checked out the
very first official selection for . . .

Library card
112764921198